# MRS. HEN
# Goes to Market

By GODFREY LYNN

Illustrated by ELIZABETH WEBBE

RAND McNALLY & COMPANY • Chicago

ONE MORNING, very early, Henrietta Hen lay in bed and opened one eye. She saw the sun just peeking over the hill. Then she heard Rooster cry, "Cock-a-doodle-doo!" and she knew it was morning.

Henrietta thought, "Everyone else is going to do something wonderful today. But I shall do the same old things I do every day—cook the breakfast, wash the dishes, sweep the floor, and go to market." And she sighed a big sigh. "I don't even want to get up!"

But she did get up. She cooked
a big corn pudding for breakfast.
Then she tied some lunch in a
red handkerchief for Rooster.

Then she shooed the children
into the garden to play.

"Same old dishes," grumbled Henrietta as she washed the dishes.

"Same old dust," she muttered as she swept the floor.

"And . . . . same old going to market," she said, reaching for her bonnet and shawl.

She picked up her pocket-book, and her shopping bag, and her umbrella, and trudged down the road to the market. And there she bought some beautiful red apples for an apple pie.

On the way home Henrietta was still grumbling, "Nothing ever happens to me," when a raindrop splashed on her nose . . . .

. . . . and the wind started to blow.
And there, overhead, was a big
black cloud.

Henrietta opened her umbrella right away because she didn't like to get wet.

No sooner had she opened it than a strong gust of wind swooped under it. She was so busy trying to hold onto the umbrella, and the pocketbook, and the shopping bag—and at the same time keep her tail feathers dry—she didn't notice that her feet had left the ground.

Then she looked down and saw that the wind was carrying her up, up into the air. "Heavens!" she gasped. "There goes my pocketbook!"

The pocketbook landed with a PLOP in Mrs. Duck's yard. "It's raining pennies!" cried Mrs. Duck.

"And there go my beautiful red apples!" said Henrietta.

The red apples fell all around Mrs. Goose below. "It's raining apples!" shouted Mrs. Goose.

Meanwhile Henrietta was being lifted higher and higher into the sky. But she was getting used to it. She even decided that it was fun to ride along in the wind. She was just thinking about enjoying the sights when—

SWOOSH! . . . .
her umbrella blew inside out.

In an instant she was drop-
ping like an arrow toward the
earth below. She saw the trees
getting nearer and nearer, and in
her fright she started to flap her
wings.

Then she noticed that she wasn't falling any more, and she flapped her wings all the harder.

"I'm flying!" she cried. "I'm a bird! Oh, this is wonderful! I shall fly, and fly, all over town!"

And she did. She flew over the
apple orchard, and over the river,
and over the cabbage patch . . . .

and she just missed the church
steeple. "Things look different
from up here," she thought.

After a while her wings began to get tired, and she began to think about going home.

Henrietta's children were still playing in the garden when her shadow crossed the grass, and they all looked up.

"It's a hawk!"
    cried one.

"It's an eagle!"
    cried another.

"It's Mamma!"
    cried the third.

Henrietta landed in the pansy
bed. Her feathers were all ruffled,
her shawl was all twisted, and
her bonnet was hanging around

her neck. But there was a happy
look on her face.

"I never would have thought
of flying!" said Henrietta.

Henrietta doesn't mind getting up in the morning any more.
She bounces out of bed clucking
a jolly little song.

She hustles with the cooking,
and hustles with the dishes—
and hustles with the sweeping.
And she just can't wait to go to
market—
because now . . . .
Henrietta FLIES to market
      every day!